IT SHOULDN'T HAPPEN TO AN AID WORKER

(*balkanski jebač*)

PROKLETIJE, LONDON

ISBN: 978-1-5272-1913-7

For Chantal, Tunicia and Benni

> "With every day, and from both sides of my intelligence, the moral and the intellectual, I thus grew steadily nearer to that truth, by whose partial discovery I have been doomed to such a dreadful shipwreck: that man is not truly one, but truly two".

Robert Louis Stephenson, *The Strange Case of Dr Jekyll and Mr Hyde*

The events described below took place between 1994 and 1997, in the Balkans, the former Soviet Union, and Africa.

I

"Genocide is inevitable once a perfect storm has been created: the victims have been absolutely demonised within and physically separated from wider society; and the enemy has them at its absolute mercy. Then all that is required is for a single voice to say 'Do it'."

She had an angelic face with pale blue eyes. At last they were alone together. The office-stroke-flat was theirs until the morning, when they would have to continue their journey south. They could relax and enjoy some time off, protected by railway sleepers leant against the windows from the shrapnel of any shells that might land outside, and he would attempt to seduce her. He had had his eye on her for some time, and suspected the feeling was mutual. But he was feeling very low physically: he had a nasty diarrhoea that had left him light-headed and weak, and demanded frequent dashes to the toilet to expel the foul, yellow liquid from his bowels. She offered to make him tea, which he gratefully accepted. The tea roused his spirits somewhat, but also provoked another series of sorties to the bathroom. Alas, the improvement in his state was only temporary, and in the end he accepted that it wasn't going to happen today. Suitably apologetic, cursing his ill luck but needing to lie down, he retired to sleep off his ill-times ailment. What the Americans call a "rain check".

In another time and place, they went on holiday together. At one Youth Hostel, they were in bunks – him up, her down. But instead of mounting his upper deck, he crept into her bower. "What are you doing?" she asked rhetorically. "Making love", he replied, kissing her. The kiss lasted and he felt her passion awake. It had been building up in both of them all day. But when he tried to remove her pyjamas, it became apparent that the bunk was simply too narrow, and not designed for such activities. After a few minutes of fruitless fumbling, he got out and, kneeling on the floor, proceeded to undress both her and himself. At last he was able to feast his eyes and then his other senses on her naked female splendour. The white voluptuousness was not quite what he had imagined, and he put out of his mind any less appetising associations. Her nipples were very small, almost lifeless, not what he'd expected from this busty blonde Teuton. Descending to her blonde pubis, he discovered her gentle hidden lips to be quite pungent as he attempted to engage with her clitoris. Nor did she seem to appreciate his ministrations, for she raised his head. Kissing her again, he made to mount her, but she instructed him to put on a condom. "I don't have any", he protested, hoping against hope that she would produce one. And with German efficiency, she did not disappoint. Rolling the rubber skin into place, he mounted her again, successfully this time. But the cramped billet did not make for a particularly memorable coupling; rather, there was plenty of banging of heads, elbows and knees, and he did not find it worthwhile to prolong the pleasure beyond the initial ecstatic surge.

She was a part-time waitress in a restaurant-stroke-bar he frequented at lunchtimes with a colleague. In conversation with her he learnt that they lived on the same street, and she invited him to come round one evening. He did so, and after some small talk intimated that he found her attractive. At his suggestion, they retired from the kitchen to the bedroom, to continue their interaction more intimately. After a while he shifted from the sitting to the lying position on the narrow bed covered with a rough blanket, implying to his hostess that she should do the same. Which she did without protest. Continuing to whisper sweet nothings in her ear, he slowly slid his arm down her thigh, and then up again, underneath her skirt. Still no protest. But when he slid his hand inside her knickers, she whispered, "I haven't had a wash". "Doesn't matter", he replied, and proceeded to gently explore the sticky warmth of her mucus membrane. It looked like he was on for it tonight. She was not reacting much, apart from falling silent; perhaps she was too nervous to relax and enjoy it. But that wasn't stopping him. Deciding it was the moment to take the plunge, he whispered "Take them off", with which she dutifully complied. He then moved on top of her, and she helpfully guided his cock inside her. Entry was not as straightforward as he might have expected, and he felt her knuckles dig into his lower abdomen as she positioned his tool and her hips. Plunging deep into her, he noted that she was still quite dry, and he started to move back and forth with regular movements, hoping to establish a rhythm that she could resonate with. Within a few moments, the edge was taken off her dryness as her vaginal fluids began to flow. Just then there was a cry of "Mama" from the other room; she replied "I'm here", and then there was silence. Her young son must have been talking in his sleep. But that was too much for him: the voice had sounded unnaturally loud in the absolute silence of the curfew night, and the fear that it might be heard by someone outside, not least her major husband who was supposed to be away fighting, made him decide it was time to go. With a few swift strokes he was ready to orgasm, and at the last moment he withdrew and spilled his hot seed on the blanket. "No!" she whispered, and quickly sat up to examine the stain. "My husband will see that!" He thought she would have appreciated the fact that he hadn't come inside her, which could have produced a far more visible result; he also thought that she should be able to clean it up with a bit of scrubbing. Quickly he pulled up and did up his trousers, and muttering a farewell greeting, exited her cottage.

They met a works dinner on a break from the warzone. He could see she was a few years older than he, but she was still very attractive, with black hair and blue eyes. After dinner they danced, and he suggested they retire to her flat. She consented, and after a 15-minute walk through the cold night air, they arrived. As soon as they had crossed the threshold and the door was closed, he embraced her and they kissed passionately. Sliding his hands down her lithe length, he lifted up her skirt and ran his hands back up to the top of her tights. She sighed and shook with pleasure. Then, with a swift movement, he pulled her tights and knickers down to below her arse. Still kissing her, he fondled and caressed her bare buttocks, and then brought one hand around to the front. Entering her overgrown valley with his fingers, he gently massaged the sacred spot, to her quiet delight. Then they went into the living room and stripped off. Her vulva was somewhat shrivelled and looked as if it had seen better days, but her anus was nice and tight as he explored it with a forefinger while thrusting his tongue into her rather wide vagina and licking out her vulva. Then it was time to release all the pressure, and he mounted her and fucked her in rapid order. Afterwards they relaxed by the light of the gas fire, with refreshment available in the form of a bottle of vodka. They discussed sexual preferences among other things, and he enquired whether she enjoyed anal sex. "Wait" she said, and went to the bathroom. She came back after what seemed like a long time later, and the she asked him to fuck her up the arse. She lay on her side with her far leg cocked, as in the recovery position, and asked him to fuck her like that. He acquiesced and, holding her with one arm under hers and on her breasts and the other up by her head, slid into her tradesman's entrance, which she had obviously lubricated while she was in the bathroom. She shuddered with delight as he began to push rhythmically into her, hoping to make her wish a true experience for her, and for him. After what seemed like an age, he decided it was time he reaped his own reward, and he began to speed up his movements, until they were both shaken by the convulsions of his orgasm. Alas, she had never mastered the art of oral sex. Her tender mouthings of his cock would have been more appropriate for thawing an ice lolly, than bringing a man to climax. But he was too polite to say so.

They met again several weeks later, and again he stayed at hers. After initial caresses aroused their passions and induced them to strip off, she crouched down on all fours on the floor and, standing behind her, he penetrated her vagina from behind. After some introductory strokes, he decided he was not happy with their relative position, and adjusted his height downwards to increase his freedom of movement. He must have found the ideal height, because as he began to thrust into her again, he was convulsed by a frenzied wave of pleasure, a pleasure that was only intensified the harder he pushed, and which was communicated to and shared by his hostess with equal intensity. Shortly thereafter he reached orgasm with a cry, and they both lay on the floor to recover. At some stage he was surprised to hear a child cry in what appeared to be the next room, and he enquired whether his hostess had a baby. "That's my daughter's baby" she informed him. The next day they went for a walk around the town and when they got back she cooked him a nice meal of steamed pork and mashed potatoes. On their way back to the flat they bumped into her daughter just going out with her baby in a pushchair. She greeted him with a smile and a tight hug, but alas, appeared not to be interested in anything any more intimate.

They met in a night club. In fact it was a colleague who first took her fancy, and then she suggested he come along for the ride. They were all on holiday from the warzone. He guessed she was a good decade older than them. In the taxi back to her flat she told them that she was a porno actress. After what seemed like an age travelling in a freezing, rickety van, they arrived. It was a nice flat, so she obviously did quite well for herself – assuming the flat belonged to her. The colleague said he would be quick about his business, and would then depart, leaving her for him. He asked for a spare condom, and then turned the couch round and asked him to stay behind it and not look over the top while he was shagging her. He looked just long enough to see her start getting undressed, and the sight of her suspender tops as she removed her shoes and then her skirt sent tremors of anticipation through him. He didn't have to wait long. Dismissing from his mind the fact that she was not fresh (and focussing on the fact that his colleague had skinned up), he quickly stripped off in turn, and embraced her with a passionate kiss. She had removed her sexy underwear and was completely naked, a very handsome, well-proportioned blonde, with dark pubic hair. He felt slightly awkward faced with the challenge of satisfying this professional Aphrodite, all the more so as he knew he would inevitably be compared to his colleague's prior performance. She appeared to enjoy his attempts to excite her with a professional indulgence, and it was perhaps due to this that in a very short time, still in the living room, he was pounding her vagina with thrusts of his rubber-bound cock. After he had finished, he asked if he could stay the night. "We've only just started" she replied, and went into the kitchen. He disposed of the condom, and then followed her into the kitchen at her invitation, where he was surprised to see she had a bottle of champagne and two glasses. But the glasses were surplus to requirements – she just drank from the bottle, with erotic gestures. She took up position on a chair, and asking him if a he wanted a drink, proceeded to pour the bubbly liquid over her breasts. At first he attempted to drink the merry libation directly from her bosom, but it quickly became apparent that that was not her intention. Heading south, he discovered that her pubic hair caused the champagne to collect, and then pass in rivulets to either side of, and down through her vulva. Eagerly he set to work lapping up this third stream, flavoured as he imagined it to be by her internal juices (and hopefully nothing else). They carried on like this for a while, which she seemed to enjoy, and then drawing her buttocks forward and lifting her legs further up he began to catch and sip the liquid as it reached her anus. An exploratory probe suggested that she was not particularly watertight, and so he hoped there might be another treat in store. Meanwhile his sexual powers had begun to return, and he invited her to perform oral sex on him in turn. Exchanging positions on the chair, she proceeded to do just that, with a professionalism that was somehow devoid of passion. Nevertheless, he let her continue until, feeling he was ready for another exertion, he suggested they exchange positions again. This time he penetrated her with his cock, and started to push in and out with an initial, gentle rhythm, hoping to incite a reciprocal movement. She played her part immaculately, although he had the sense that she was not experiencing any real pleasure. After reaching a plateau of delight, he withdrew, and lowering himself a degree, attempted to enter her anus. "I'm saving that for my husband" she said, and guided his member back into its natural home. He continued to thrust in and out of her rhythmically, wondering when it would be appropriate to expend his second wind in the presence of this worldly-wise nymphomaniac. To spice things up, he suggested she turn round, and they began to fuck from behind. Now he was getting into his stride, and after a few minutes, he came inside her with a spasmodic, voiced shudder. She suggested they had a shower together to wash off, to which he agreed. Afterwards he asked her what her plans were for the next day (which was fast approaching). "I'm filming" she replied. "Can I come?" he asked. "Of course" she confirmed generously. His head spinning, he persisted; "Can I join in?" "No problem" she promised. She was not displaying any signs of fatigue, and so he suggested they catch 40 winks and then perhaps have another round of passion. She consented to this, and before he knew it he was fast asleep. When they awoke in the morning, she said they were late and would have to leave immediately. Quickly they got dressed and emerged into the morning sunlight, and she immediately hailed a taxi and gave him an address that meant nothing to him. He had only been in the city for a few days. As they drove along, and as his befuddled mind began to return to a form of sober consciousness, he began to wonder what he had let himself in for. He had no idea where they were going, no idea who would be there, and no real idea about what they would be getting up to. Maybe he would be the one getting fucked this time? Nor did anyone know where he was. As they approached a tube station, he made up his mind, and telling the driver to stop, said goodbye to his lover and got out. He never saw her again.

There were four of them in the sleeper compartment, a middle-aged man whom he didn't regard as competition, and two young ladies off to their summer quarters on the coast. Would their professional pride preclude a nocturnal fling? It certainly wasn't the Oriental Express. Technically they weren't at work yet. He ended up in one of the top bunks, with the girl he fancied most in the bunk below him. Everyone turned out their bedside lights except her, and silently he crept down into her space. "What are you doing?" she asked quietly, to which he began to whisper sweet nothings into her ear, all the while trying to turn off the light. But he couldn't get it to go off, and his attempts to establish a beautiful friendship ran up against a brick wall.

II

"As the only creatures capable of abstract thought, symbols are the currency with which we are bought and sold. Communication is the most powerful tool in the highest ape's arsenal, for it can override an interlocutor's reason and harness his or her potential. The master of symbols is the master of the destiny of nations. But the sleight of hand does not last forever: the laws of physics can be bent, but will not be broken."

He was on R&R away from the warzone. They had been introduced by a mutual acquaintance, and she consented to accompany him home. "Do you have hot water?" she enquired. Alas, the boiler was out of order, and so she had to have a cold shower before they got to grips with each other. When she returned with a towel around her, he was already naked on the bed. He removed her towel, and they kissed passionately. Pushing him onto his back, she mounted him backwards and began to perform fellatio. Her arsehole was staring at him like Aladdin's cave. But would he find the password? He reciprocated with a will, despite the fact that her vulva was still cold from the shower. Her pubic hair was a prickly stubble, she must have shaved recently. After a short while his efforts managed to warm up her genitals, and he began to explore her third eye with his tongue. Then something unexpected happened: despite his determination to delay climax until they had both thoroughly enjoyed themselves, he suddenly found himself in the grip of a powerful orgasm, an experience that made his head swim for an instant and elicited an animal cry of pleasure. "How did you do that?" he asked her a few moments later, to which she just laughed shyly, as she washed his seed down with a swig of vodka. As they lay resting, they soon began to feel the cold, and so they cuddled up under the blanket. Before too long his sexual energy returned, and they shagged again, at length, in the missionary position. Then he turned over and bid her crouch over him so that he could fuck her vertically. She did as he asked, but when she tried to place his rubber-coated cock into herself, she found the condom to be an impediment. "Can I take it off?" she asked, to which he assented. That was better: it just slid in of its own accord, and he was treated to the full sensation of her inner sanctum as she moved up and down his cock, first slowly and then with increased vigour until, grasping her by the hips, he took over the controls as he orgasmed deep into her.

They met at a restaurant at lunch time. He was seated opposite her and her husband at a communal trestle table, and they struck up a conversation. When the husband went to the bathroom, she slipped him a piece of paper with a phone number and told him to call her in half an hour. She wasn't quite an oil painting, but her forthright approach intrigued him. Quickly thereafter, when the husband came back, he finished his meal, paid his bill, and left, his mouth dry with anticipation. At the allotted time he made the call from a phone box, and they agreed to meet up at a certain place half an hour later. When they were reunited, they wasted no time in taking a taxi back to his digs. Upon entering, he sat down on a chair and she stood beside him, caressing his hair and radiating the whore's happiness. Not feeling particularly talkative, rather than enter into small talk he simply lifted up her skirt to inspect her wares, before telling her to undress. She did so with a smile, as did he, and they retired to the bed. Getting to know each other with their mouths, he explored her rather plump body and ended up between her legs. By a quirk of fate, one of his front teeth was loose, and as he was exploring the entrance to her vagina with his tongue, his tooth came free and slipped up the waiting orifice. Fortunately it came back out again of its own accord, and he was able without much trouble to return it temporarily to its place without her noticing. He then enjoined on her to perform a similar act on him, which she proceeded to do. But she did not have a particularly magic touch, and before long she stopped, complaining that it was too much for her jaw muscles, which had started to ache. He then pushed his cock into her fanny and they began to have sex in the missionary position, to her delight. Having achieved a certain level of pleasure from these activities, he exited and turned her over before penetrating her again. But this time she began to complain again, because she said it was too much of a strain on her legs. Starting to lose patience, he returned her to her former position, in which they continued to fornicate with increasing intensity until he reached orgasm.

They met in a bar on his first night in transit through the town to the warzone. They were introduced by a mutual acquaintance, one of his colleagues, and they immediately struck up a conversation. She was exceptionally beautiful, verging on the voluptuous but not overweight, with a charming smile, and they seemed to hit it off right away. Beyond her physical charms, he was struck by the open and frank yet thoughtful way in which she expressed herself. At the end of the evening he invited her to come home with him, to which she assented without hesitation. The only place in the house where they would have any privacy was in the garage, which contained a camp bed. It was also quite cold, and so they snuggled up naked under the blanket, he warming her from behind until their animal heat induced them to become more active. The restricted space afforded by the camp bed prevented him from engaging in some of the more extensive foreplay that was his want; but the raging fire in his loins that was making his head swim allowed him to easily overlook that omission. He felt the sweat welling up at the points where their bodies touched as he caressed her rounded body and kissed her on the neck and cheeks from behind. Then, as if by unanimous decision, she spun round and they kissed passionately. On her lips and tongue he could taste the first realisation of the promise of their first encounter, even as he continued to explore the rest of her body with his left hand; and she began to gently wank him off. Not wishing to stand on ceremony, he prepared to mount her; but she insisted on a condom. Quickly he retrieved one from her handbag and knelt over her while she fitted it, and then they resumed their prostrate positions on the trusty old camp bed as he penetrated her. He was so consumed with desire that he was afraid he might not be able to hold back for long, but with a supreme effort of the will and the occasional halt he was able to pace his performance until he felt from the rhythm of her hips that they were of one mind and spirit. Finally, he let himself go into a frenzied frenzy of ejaculation, dimly aware of cries of pleasure in his ears. They slept fitfully on their narrow berth, and waking up early, just had time for another round of heavenly passion before she had to leave to go to work.

They met up again the next evening in the same bar, and this time they agreed they would retire to her place. They took a taxi and walked the last few yards over her landlady's garden to the door of her bedsit; she urging him to be quite so that her landlady wouldn't notice him, while he was already imagining and planning his order of battle, his style no longer cramped by restricted quarters. As soon as they were inside the door, he turned her to him and began to kiss her passionately, and then, unable to wait, he knelt down with her on the bed, lifted her skirt, removed her knickers, and began to kiss her swollen, damp vulva. She sighed with pleasure as he carefully and strategically devoted his charms now to her clitoris, now to the smooth channel that lies beneath, occasionally thrusting his tongue deep into the magical folds of her vagina. After a while she lifted him up, and quickly undressing, produced a condom. He rapidly followed suit, and she unrolled the rubber shield down his cock. He mounted her and entered, and immediately they began to make love, he endeavouring to make his exertions last, while she encouraged him with exhortations of "Fuck me!" He had initially planned to fuck her from behind after these initial manoeuvres, but he was so turned on he could no longer hold himself back, and began to pound into her with all his concentrated might, his head swimming until his juices dried up. They talked for a while and then fell asleep; and in the morning, they once again engaged in a semi-conscious round of juicy, sensual fucking.

They had become quite friendly, more than acquaintances, but no opportunity for a more intimate encounter had presented itself. She was one of the most beautiful women he had ever seen, voluptuous and sultry, but with a shy smile. She was a waitress in a café he sometimes frequented at lunchtimes with a colleague when on breaks from the warzone. Then, on the evening of a fair, their paths crossed at the periphery of someone else's conversation. "Me and you" she said, gesturing to suggest that they should get to know each other better. "Come on then", he replied, and she joined him. But he was just recovering from malaria and had been struggling with diarrhoea that afternoon and evening, which wasn't helped by the beers he had consumed; and just as she joined him, he sneezed. The involuntary spasm that traversed his body had an unwelcome and unexpected side effect, causing his careful grip on his sphincter to not only relax, but to be superseded by a downward explosive force as his bowels evacuated fluid. They travelled back with the rest of the group in the direction of the hotel, he in a state of optimistic misery. In the hotel room, he bid his guest relax while he retired apologetically to the bathroom, hoping to make himself presentable without unreasonable delay. Stripping off, he placed the soiled garments in the sink to be dealt with once he had washed his body clean. He then stepped into the bath tub and started to rinse himself down. "Are you alright?" she called from the bedroom. "Yes, I'll just be a minute" he replied, and continued his ritual cleansing. Suddenly the door opened, and she walked in, naked apart from a string of beads around her waist. She was like a goddess, a strong-limbed black Amazon. "I still have to clean my underwear" he stammered, but disregarding his concerns, she stepped into the bath with him. "I'll do that later" she undertook generously and, squatting down, took his cock in her mouth. Her knees were apart and her hands on his hips as she began to take his member in and out of her gullet. The sudden change in his fortune sent a spasm through his being, and he was almost overcome by pleasure. Lifting her up hurriedly (after ensuring he was properly clean), he said "Come on", and led her into the bedroom. After a quick, passionate kiss, he started to explore her breasts, her stomach, and her fanny with his mouth. But, impatiently, she pulled him back upwards, and they began to fuck. Already halfway there, it wasn't long before he was filling her with waves of spunk. He pulled away and rolled over onto his back, the sheets in disarray, his hand resting on her stomach. After he had recovered his composure, he remembered the unfinished business in the bathroom, and made to go back there. "I'll do it" she interrupted him, and as good as her word, did so. There was another round of semi-conscious ecstasy in the middle of the night; and in the morning when he got up, he was gratified to see a string of his spunk stretching out of her vagina, the brilliant white set off against the jet black skin and curly body hair.

Several weeks later they met again, and returned to the same hotel. After they had entered, she took to the staircase that led to the room they had shared on the previous occasion. She was wearing a short yellow dress that was driving him mad with the thought of lifting it up and exploring the delights hidden beneath, and which provided a tantalising glimpse of those very promises as she walked up in front of him. "Not that way" he said, as this time they were in a room on the ground floor. Passing through the door, he chaperoned her onto the bed and, lifting up her dress and removing her knickers, penetrated her immediately from behind. After a few moments of ecstatic and energetic thrusting, in which grunts and gasps were echoed by the slap of skin smacking against skin and the squelch of vaginal fluids, it was all over. At least for now. Music could be heard from a nightclub on the other side of the road, and they decided to go back out and enjoy an evening of dance and song. Several hours later, suitably refreshed, and in merry spirits, they returned to the hotel for a more measured and leisurely intimate encounter. As soon as they entered the room, they both stripped off and, he lying on his back, she positioned herself on top of him and took his cock into her mouth. The sensation was heavenly as her head slowly moved up and down; but due to their earlier activities, he found he could not reciprocate, because her vulva tasted of his spunk. Instead, he encouraged her to sit astride him. As she crouched above him and slid his cock inside herself, he felt as though he were in heaven. Slowly she moved up and down his slippery pole, her weight borne by her legs and occasionally using her hands to balance, such that their genitalia were joined in the freedom of weightlessness. All he could feel was the mouth of her vagina as it rode slowly up and down him. After a while it became too much and he grabbed her hips and started to pound upwards into her, to which she reciprocated, lowering her knees to the bed. Finally he spun over, taking care not to exit the joyous orifice, and ploughed into her to orgasm in the classical missionary position.

She was a very elegant lady, perhaps slightly his senior, with whom he had had business earlier that day. In the evening he went out for a drink, and happened to run into her in a bar. After some small talk, she invited him back to her flat, which was part of the same building. They went straight into the bedroom, in which she appeared to sleep on a mat on the floor. Kneeling on the floor as he stood against the wall, she undid his trousers. Her confident methodical gestures combined with the calm, knowing expression on her beautiful, enigmatic face inspired in him a raging desire that made his head spin, and ensured for a powerful hard-on. His initial idea was that, after he had enjoyed the care of her lips and tongue for a while, he would fuck her on the sleeping mat. But as she began to take periodic, measured gulps of him, her lips running down his cock while her tongue caressed him like an afterthought, he noticed that she was undoing her shirt and gently caressing one breast with her right hand. Her eyes had closed in an inner ecstasy, as she began to settle into a sexual rhythm of her own. Alas, it was not to enjoy a denouement, because this combined assault on his senses was too much for his fevered brain, and he orgasmed deep into her mouth, to her evident satisfaction. They agreed to meet again in the near future, and sated, he left.

III

"Consumerism is when we are merely sold our God-given birth rights in a gift-wrapped, empty box, that makes us complicit in ruthless exploitative practices whose ugly face is carefully kept at arm's length and will rarely intrude on our personal space."

One day he was informed that the cook was intrigued by him, and wanted him to fuck her. He found her pretty, but thus far his efforts at flirting appeared to have fallen on stony ground. He had had to admire her rear end raised provocatively (as it seemed to him) into the air as she bent over her domestic tasks from afar. But now his luck appeared to have changed, although she was engaged, and so it had to be a strictly safe sex affair, by the book. Belt and braces. At the appointed day and time, he was told she was waiting for him in the living room. He went in, and found her sitting on the sofa, fully clothed. "Are you still on for this?" he enquired. "Yes" she replied, "I'm ready, have you got a condom?" Dutifully he produced one, and was instructed to put it on. Undoing his trousers and doing just that, he sat down beside her. She had a close look to make sure it was watertight, and then invited him to lift up her skirt and enter her. Slightly perplexed, but aroused, he did just that: getting close to her, he slid his hands under her skirt and then positioned his loins next to where he guessed hers must be. She then decided to give him a helping hand and, adjusting her hips in order to be in position, she guided his cock inside her. Then she sat back again and waited, their entwined genitalia hidden from view. Slightly nonplussed, he tried to kiss her, but she pulled her head back. He decided there was nothing for it but to move into first gear, and began to push against her, rocking in and out of her vagina. She was quite dry, and didn't seem to lubricate with his efforts, although the changing expressions on her docile, taciturn face indicated to him that he was at least having an effect. The baggy plastic bag around his cock wasn't helping. After a few minutes of this he decided he wasn't getting anywhere, and that it was time to engage the turbo. Leaning onto her and grasping her, he threw caution to the winds, and within a few thrusting strokes shot his load. "Have you finished?" she asked. In answer, he withdrew, whereupon she insisted on giving the condom a thorough visual inspection to make sure it hadn't leaked. Altogether a very curious encounter, which was not repeated.

She came to his room, looking for a colleague. He never asked her name, but bid her undress and did the same. Nor could he speak her language. She had silken skin and beautiful breasts, the nipples pointing forward horizontally. As he began to enjoy her body in his accustomed fashion, her overwhelming sense seemed to be curiosity. He guessed that she had never been with a foreigner before. In particular, as he lavished his oral affections on her nether regions, she was leaning forward to observe his every move. Nevertheless, they achieved a meeting of minds as he entered her in the missionary position, and after a few strokes he achieved a tremulous orgasm, to their mutual satisfaction.

He ended up with both of them in the one room, with a double bed. They stripped off, and at first he encouraged them to engage in the classical lesbian activities, something they were loath to do. So he centred his attentions on the one he had met first, who was also the largest of the two. In fact she had originally been with his colleague, who had bottled out at the last minute. His thinking was to use her for a warm up, and then expend his second wind on her more attractive companion at a more leisurely pace. He explored her mouth, breasts and fanny with his tongue, and then entered her with his cock. Having already consumed several beers, it was not long before he had orgasmed into her, and he then rolled over and fell asleep, as the other lady had already done. In the middle of the night he awoke with a hard-on and, turning to the more petite of the two, started to lavish his attentions on her. She was by far the prettier of the two, and there was something in her eyes that had initially conveyed to him that a certain animal chemistry could be established between them, a compound resulting from their physical proximity that would be more than mere coupling. She awoke to his tender caresses with a look of lust in her eyes. She was truly beautiful, although in the light of the table lamp she had insisted on leaving on he noticed that she had major stretch marks extending the full length of her body. But as he kissed her breasts, suddenly his mouth was invaded by a warm, sweet substance, that he recognised immediately from his earliest childhood. "Have you got a baby?" he asked. "How do you know?" she countered. Putting these concerns aside, he mounted her, and thrusting and pushing to his heart's content, achieved a very satisfactory orgasm.

He had seen her before, at an evening's drinks, and they had caught each other's eye. She was very petite and pretty. A few weeks later, he had gone into an establishment looking for a toilet, and she happened to be there. She said she would show him where the toilet was. Suspecting she had something else in mind, he quickly grew a stiff hard-on, which was rather uncomfortable as he was dying for a piss. But he followed her to a door, and went in. Opening his trousers he pulled out his cock, and tried to think of England in an attempt to induce it to subside so that he could relieve himself. But he hadn't noticed that she was loitering at the door, and when she saw his cock she came into the toilet, knelt down and started to suck it. He couldn't believe it, and was both gratified and put out at her initiative. But his colleague was waiting for him outside, and he decided he had to put a stop to this impromptu intimacy. Stepping back, he gently encouraged her to leave, and after his passions had momentarily subsided, he was able to complete his business. On the way out she was waiting for him, and they agreed to meet that evening at a cheap, sleazy hotel opposite his shared digs. Trembling with anticipation and elation, he returned to his colleague who was patiently waiting for him in the car, and told him what had happened. That evening, his throat dry and contracted so that he found it difficult to speak, and his vision blurring from the desire of what was to come, they met up as planned. She had already organised the room, and as soon as they went entered it they stripped off. She was very slight, with small breasts and a sparse goatee above a quite insubstantial vulva. They kissed and embraced, and he proceeded to explore her body from closer at hand, lavishing the best efforts of his lips and tongue on her breasts, stomach, and then her fanny. But it seemed so undeveloped that he found he was unable to gain a suitable traction, and after a few minutes attempting to elicit a passionate response from her clitoris, he went to enter her. Quickly she produced a condom and rolled it on. Then he entered her; but her vagina was so tight, and she was so light, that again he was unable to establish a satisfactory rhythm. But she seemed to be enjoying herself, and so he let himself go and slowly started to move in and out of her as he began to feel the heady power of lust return to his being. The gentle odour of her sweat in his nostrils only added to the intoxication that had taken possession of him. Before he knew it, the end was nigh, and he grabbed her hips and thrust into her until he had finished orgasming into the latex rubber capsule. Relieved, he lay on his back while she sat beside him, cheerful and chatty. She told him there was a bath full of water for washing in the bathroom, and he went there to get cleaned up. But the evening was so hot, and he was already sweaty and dirty from his day's work, that the drab, rather short, bare concrete tub of water looked inviting, and he got in. It was cold, but that was what he wanted, and stretching his head back and his feet forward and up onto the opposite edge, he just lay there, in a heaven of sorts. After a few minutes she came to see what had happened to him, and was surprised to see what he was up to. He invited her to join him, which she did; but it was so cold she quickly got out again and said she would wait for him on the bed. When he was suitable refreshed, and began to feel his balls turn to ice, he got out, dried off, and rejoined her. This time they embarked upon a more leisurely round of lovemaking. Laying her on her back, he began to lick her out with more purposeful resolve, determined that she should enjoy the full range of his skills. She seemed to appreciate his care and persistence, and began to indicate by small movements and sounds that the was connecting with her inner sanctum. Raising her legs, he spread her buttocks apart so that he could transfer his attentions to her arsehole, which she also appeared to appreciate. But it was a tightly-sealed mystery, practically out of sight, and so he resumed his degustation of her vulva and clitoris. After a while, he felt his passions arousing again, and decided it was time for another penetration. But she protested that she didn't have any more condoms, and didn't want to have full sex without one. What to do? He suggested she finish off what she had started earlier that day in the toilet, and lying back, relaxed as she clambered on top of him and, spreading her small buttocks just in front of his chin, she started to suck his cock, deeply and rhythmically. At first he attempted to complement her efforts by lavishing more of his oral efforts on her nether regions; but before long, the pleasure he was feeling started to overwhelm him, and he lay back. Soon thereafter he orgasmed into her mouth, grasping her buttocks as he rocked his hips into her face. She continued until he had completely subsided. Then he had to go back to his digs, for a colleague had called him on the radio asking where he was.

Several years later they met again by pure chance, in a nightclub. But she was now with her husband, and they confined their encounter to polite small talk.

She joined him at his table at a bar where he was relaxing one evening after a long day's work. Politely, he encouraged her to sit, and bought her a drink, but she was not much of a conversationalist. She was very pretty, perhaps his own age. After a while he suggested they leave, to her place, because he was sharing a room with a female colleague who might not have appreciated a third party presence. After walking about half an hour, to an area he was unfamiliar with, but from where he was confident he would be able to find his way back, they entered a house. She led him to a bedroom and bade him lie down, while she went into another room. He heard a brief whispered conversation, and perhaps a male voice, and then she came back and lay down beside him. He kissed her, and they started to embrace. In no time they were naked, and he began to explore her well-proportioned body in the near-darkness with all his senses. Exploring her vulva with his tongue, he gently probed her anus with his forefinger, and was surprised when it slipped right in with no difficulty. It seemed to be lubricated; but with what? Re-ascending her supine form, he mounted her, and slid his cock into her vagina. A few strokes were sufficient to achieve a level of pleasure that he hoped was mutual, but he held off completing his task. His hands now level with his face, he was able to verify without making it obvious that there were no odours of sewage emanating from his forefinger. Remembering what he had encountered down below, he withdrew his cock and, repositioning himself, attempted to slide it into the abominable Holy Grail. To his delight and surprise, and to a grunt from his companion, it slipped right in! He was now in his element and, giving free rein to his passions in this variation on the missionary position, he fucked her hard until he orgasmed deep into her guts.

They became acquaintances, if not friends, and one evening he invited round to his flat. Impressing on her the need for silence, he led her into the bedroom and they stripped off. They kissed and embraced passionately, and as he did the rounds of her erogenous zones with his hands and mouth, the warmth of her body and its gentle scents sent his head spinning. This time the light was on, and he was able to get a much better look at her in all her glory. Her small breasts and slim hips were a perfect match to her beautiful eyes, nose and mouth, and sitting dormant but latent in his embrace, the sight began to make his head swim. Without further ado he entered her vagina and began to move her with rhythmic thrusts, now gentle, now more violent. But he was still curious about her other orifice, and exiting from her genitals, he pushed his cock up her arse. Again it entered without difficulty, and produced only a slight change in her reaction. After establishing a rhythm again, he withdrew once more, and turned her over. This time he entered her from behind, first vaginally, and then anally. The sight of her smooth, rounded buttocks pressed right against his loins, the smooth crack merging with his body hair as he rocked her back and forth against him, was a powerful aphrodisiac, and saving himself as long as he could, he eventually gave way to an orgasm that elicited an animal shout. Relaxing on the bed afterwards, he hoped his flatmate hadn't heard.

"Why do you keep putting it up there?" She asked. "Why, don't you like it?" he asked in turn, to which she just shrugged. In the morning they sneaked quietly into the bathroom together, carrying their clothes. As he brushed his teeth, she sat on the toilet, still naked, to piss. Seized by a thought, he directed his cock towards his face in the hope that she would suck him off, but she turned her head away. She knew where it had been.

IV

"Organised religion is the heroin of the masses. The unforgiving singularity of the desert allows for no deviance."

He had seen her working at the cholera laundry, and they had shared a few snatched conversations between breaks. What he liked most about her was her sincere, patient smile, which gave her already pretty face a radiant beauty. He told her where he was staying and invited her to come round on Sunday afternoon. He didn't expect her to, but that Sunday he happened to be at home in the afternoon when there was a knock. He opened the door and sure enough it was her, with a friend. He invited them into his Spartan digs and they all sat on the bed. Her friend was not particularly attractive, but she had a good figure, and she was so much darker than their mutual acquaintance that they complemented each other strikingly, in a manner that suggested erotic promise. He also thought he detected in her eyes a complicity, as of things to come not yet spoken of. To his great shame, he had no refreshments to offer them, and this disgraceful failing sapped his confidence, such that he felt unable to take full advantage of the situation.

He was staying at a colleague's house in his and his family's absence in a different town over the weekend. It was winter and quite cold. There was a live-in housekeeper, who he had met briefly before, and who he remembered had cast him some not unsympathetic glances. In the evening, alone in the house, they started to talk. At a certain moment on the way back from the toilet they passed each other in the corridor, and how he was not quite sure, but they kissed. With a smile they began to passionately embrace, and continued to explore each other's lips and tongues. Then she crouched down and, with a little help from him, extracted his cock. Inexpertly, she began to perform what she thought would excite him; but he just waited for her to finish, too polite to tell her to stop. Suddenly he heard the sound of children coming through the front door: it was her children, a boy and a girl. "Stop", he said, "the kids!" "Never mind them" she replied, and took another mouthful of his penis. This was too much for him, and he quickly withdrew and, turning his back, did up his trousers just as the children came into the corridor. "Follow me" she instructed, and led him through a door into what was clearly their shared bedroom. She closed the door, stripped off, and produced a condom. "Don't you want to?" she asked, upon which he undid his trousers again, and she unrolled the rubber onto his hard-on. Then she crept onto the bed and bent over, so that her backside was sticking up in the air, pointing at him. Following her cue, he took up position standing behind her, and pushed his cock into her viscous sex organ. He let out a sigh, and began to push into her with hard, rhythmic strokes, grasping her arse cheeks with both hands. But he didn't want it to end so soon, and withdrawing, he bent down behind her and began to explore her vulva with his tongue. She emitted more soft sounds as he became familiar with the gateway to her sanctum, and then, straightening up and pulling her buttocks apart slightly, he transferred his attentions to her anus. It was an ideal position for such an activity, as the third eye was looking straight up at him, and she seemed more than happy with this turn of events. Deciding to take the plunge, he straightened up and attempted to force his cock into that darkest of holes. But he seemed to be pushing against a solid wall, despite her attempts to improve her position so as to facilitate his manoeuvre, and the fabric of the condom appeared to be more a hindrance than a help. But just then he heard the children outside the door; it appeared their entrance was imminent, and he jumped away quickly and pulled up his trousers. "I don't believe it" she said, covering herself as the kids came in. That was the end of that.

They met again some time later, but were never able to finish what they had started.

He met her in a night club on his way out of the warzone. Or rather, she foisted himself on him: at first she thrust something into his hand, which he immediately dropped, fearing it was an illegal substance. Then she accosted him directly, insisting that he take her back to his hotel (and that she had merely been attempting to give him her telephone number). She was wearing a bright red dress, which lent her a striking appearance, but she was somewhat overweight, such that her appearance verged on the ridiculous. After some hesitations, he agreed to humour her, and they retired to his digs. There they entered into a game of cat and mouse, for she insisted they could not have sex for religious reasons; but she was nevertheless intrigued by him as a foreigner. Putting on some loud music, they engaged in some passionate kissing on the couch, and he eventually managed to get her out of her garish kit. She was attractive in her own way, and he began to feel the flames of desire consume his reason. Then she insisted on having a shower, which they both did – separately. After they had finished, they sat naked and talked on the bed, because she was once again reticent. She questioned him on his sexual practices, and whether he always used a condom. After a while, she asked him whether he would perform oral sex on her. He assented, but insisted that they warm up by engaging in some foreplay first. He found her kisses rather stilted, and immediately began to give the rest of her body his attentions. Her large breasts were not particularly memorable, but her bearded inner sanctum appeared to offer more promise. However, when he knelt down on the ground and pulled her to the edge of the bed in order to be able to explore her genitals, she locked her legs together, once again citing holy writ. After some cajoling, she relented and relaxed her grip, although she reiterated that they could not have full sex. He attempted to explore her vulva, but once again she tensed up her thighs, such that his room to manoeuvre was extremely limited; although the limited movements his tongue was able to effectuate inside her, his teeth almost clenched against her pubic hair, seemed to meet with her approval. But after some minutes of this, he decided it was time to get real, and standing, up, he thrust his cock into the tight gap between her outer lips where his face had just been. "No!" she said, and once again her thighs locked up around him; but she made no attempt to push him away. He was now torn between the urge to do what came naturally to them both, but potentially expose himself to criminal charges; or to simply give up on a bad job.

By way of compromise he maintained his position, seeking by thrusting movements to stimulate her clitoris with his cock, and she seemed to appreciate his gallant efforts, as her eyes closed and she departed into a world of ecstasy of her own, but she made no concessions to indicate she wanted penetration. After a while he grew tired of this nonsensical game, and withdrawing completely, lay down beside her with his back to her, and bid her good night.

They were reunited by mutual acquaintances. After dinner they returned to her digs, and she stripped off to her knickers. He sat beside her and they talked, but as he had no condoms, he was reluctant to take full advantage of what appeared to be her willingness to re-engage. But neither could he tear himself away, and his voice began to tremble as he began to caress her and became more and more excited, while explaining to her his dilemma. "Why don't you take your knickers off as well?" he suggested finally, and she did so. This time she had shaved off all her pubic hair. The sight was almost too much for him, and as if on cue, she asked him if he would like a blow job. Standing up, he dropped his trousers, and she took his cock into his mouth, holding him on both hips. The pleasure was so intense that he was unable to resist it for long, and he soon orgasmed deep into her mouth. She had exerted such pressure on his penis that he could feel her efforts all the rest of the evening, and the following morning.

They started to meet up regularly in the evenings and at weekends. She was now working as a hairdresser. Getting to know each other's bodies and appetites again was a pleasure in itself. Fuelled by Johnnie Walker they caressed and kissed each other all over, gradually augmenting the level of intensity they were feeling. One evening she bade him lie on his back with his legs spread out, and she sat in front of him, her legs folded over his, and holding her ankles with her arms under his legs. She then bent forward and proceeded to deliver one of the most intense blowjobs he had ever experienced, using the grip on her ankles as an anchor to allow her to rock back and forward, and her mouth to go up and down from the root of his cock to his bell-end, and continuing well after he had shot a powerful orgasm down her throat. He asked her where she had learnt to do that, to which she just replied, "Never mind". On another occasion, an hour or so after they had made love in the afternoon, he felt his strength return. They were still naked in the bedroom, but she was occupied with something else. Calling her name, he indicated by holding his erect cock that he was back in business. She came back over and, lying on her front, proceeded to suck him. As it was his second wind, he knew he would be able to make the pleasure last, and he did just that. As she continued to patiently work on his cock, he leant over and, spreading her buttocks, started to explore her beautiful third eye with his tongue. This activity went on for what seemed like a long time until, looking for closure, they broke off only to re-engage in the standard fashion, albeit from behind. Wrapping his arms around her, he alternatively hugged and caressed her as he started to thrust into her, enjoying the elusive but evocative scent of her body, the touch of her hair against his face, and the smooth contours of her perfect body. The stores of pleasure that had been building up over the last half hour or so suddenly began to break loose, and he achieved a liberating orgasm. His cock, somewhat overworked, was rather tender for the next day or two.

They met in a night club, and he assented to accompany her home. She was pretty and voluptuous, and quite forward. He didn't have the use of a vehicle, and so she suggested they take a motorbike-taxi. Perched on the pillion seat, his hands around his new friend while she clung to the driver in front of her, it occurred to him that his health insurance might be invalidated if they came a cropper. Finally they entered her digs and stripped off. They started by kissing passionately, and before he knew it he was exploring her fulsome breasts, her stomach, and her genitals with his tongue. He lay down on top of her, face downwards, in order to have a more panoramic view of her nether regions, and to better negotiate their hidden delights, at the same time facilitating her skilful and generous attentions to his cock. Slowly he explored her smooth hidden pathway, from the tantalising hardness of her clitoris, teased out of its nest, down the smooth slipway to the entrance to her vagina, with its further hidden depths holding the promise of the world as he thrust his tongue into her yielding folds, and finally further south to that more unnatural entrance. Her anus responded to his caresses, yielding as if in invitation, but when he asked her whether she would like him to fuck her up the arse, she replied she had never done that before. At that moment her flatmate came in, and stripping off, lay down beside them with her back towards them; but as no-one else appeared to be inhibited, he decided to move into top gear as he was. Letting go of all restraints, he started to plunge rhythmically into her mouth, at the same time bestowing oral caresses on her nether regions in the form of a counterpoint. Within a few minutes he became aware of a muffled cry of delight as he let himself go into a full orgasm. Spent, he turned over onto his back, and the two of them lay there for a while, catching their breath. "Got what you wanted then?" the flatmate asked his new friend, to which she replied something he didn't catch. He stretched out his hand and caressed the flatmate, who sat up and turned around to reveal the most splendid breasts he had seen since he was 13. The nipples were large, almost like crumpets at their base, while their tips pointed boldly forward. A conversation started, while he slowly caught his second wind. Once he was back on form, he sat up as well, and started to suck the flatmate's breasts, his mouth still tasting of vaginal fluids. From time to time he sat back to admire her well-proportioned figure, and concluded that she was a truly exceptional beauty. After a while he bade her lie down and he went down on her, to discover that her vulva and anus lived up to the promise of her upper half. She seemed slightly shy in front of her friend, unable to let herself go, and so, pulling his sole condom from his wallet, he skinned up and entered her. He started off with a regular rhythm, hoping to reassure her and coax her into shedding her inhibitions, while at the same time husbanding his own resources. After a while she seemed to give way to his efforts, and reciprocate his hip movements with thrusts of her own. His first friend had lit a cigarette and seemed to be lost in a world of her own. Then he felt the madness seize his brain and cloud his vision, and stepping up a gear, he was soon letting off a second ejaculation.

V

"Refugees are the product of a failure by national and international power structures to protect society. They have no rights and no voice. Human rights and fundamental freedoms have become a Marie-Antoinette-like euphemism peddled by a feudal elite."

In a nightclub he went to the toilet, and as he pushed open the cubicle door, he was surprised to hear a female protest. There was a young lady perched on the bog, but when she saw him, she told him to come in and close the door. He did so, and after a few introductory remarks she stood up and pulled her trousers up, leaving the way clear for him to relieve himself. His business done, they both returned to the dance floor from where, after a fun evening, they retired to the house he was living in. She wasn't his usual cup of tea, somewhat on the plump side of voluptuous, but pretty, and anyway she was the best option he had had that night. Once in the bedroom, they kissed passionately standing up, and holding her head with both hands he was seized by a desire to pour all his passion into those luscious lips. Stripping off rapidly, he indicated to her to move downwards, and offered her his erect cock as a substitute for his mouth. She granted his wish, and began to enthusiastically if inexpertly take his cock in and out of her mouth. Soon he decided that it was time he got to grips with the rest of her and, stepping back and indicating to her to strip off likewise, he retired to the bed. She followed him, and he got her to sit on top of him, where she could continue to practice her fellatio while he reciprocated. The inside of her vulva and vagina was pink and juicy like a tropical fruit inside its dark envelope, and he set to work with a will with his mouth, seeking to provoke tremors of pleasure through her body. After a while he shifted position to transfer his attentions to her anus, only to discover that in contrast to its neighbour, it was dark, almost black in colour. The two orifices were like flowers in a rose garden perfectly choreographed by a divine landscape gardener. Her arsehole yielded to his efforts, opening slightly to allow his tongue to enter, and he decided it was time for penetration. Getting up, he asked her whether she would like him to fuck her up the arse, to which she said she would try anything once. However, when he attempted to enter her from behind, he found her to be far tighter than he had expected, and she quickly pulled away, changing her mind. Never mind. Resorting to plan B, he quickly extracted a condom from the wallet in his trouser pocket on the floor, pulled it on, and in no time they were enjoying straight sex, albeit from behind. He caressed and grasped her smooth body from all sides as he drove into her with increasing enjoyment, until they were both shaken by his throes of ecstasy. She stayed the night, and he drove her home in the morning. In conversation she told him she was bisexual, as she had been seduced by a woman from the UN when she was younger.

He was back in town for just one night, and climbing into a taxi, headed for bar where they had met. When he entered he saw that it had changed a bit, not for the better, and he was immediately subjected to the not universally friendly scrutiny of many of the patrons, and indeed staff. But there was no sign of his friend. He ordered a beer and sat down, hoping to mind his own business until he had got his bearings. Immediately a girl approached him and asked for a beer. She didn't want to take no for an answer, and so he agreed to buy her one, at which she sat down beside him. She was quite pretty, but very forward, and she proceeded to chat him up very aggressively. Meanwhile, a girl at another table had caught his eye, and he began to exchange furtive glances with her whenever the one-sided conversation he was involved in closer at hand permitted. Eventually his companion announced that she was going to the bathroom, and that when she returned, she knew a quiet place they could repair to. He grunted a non-committal response; but as soon as she was gone, the much more friendly-looking girl from the other table joined him. "You should watch out" she warned him, "she keeps a gun in her handbag, she plans to get you alone somewhere and then rob you. Let's leave now before she comes back". This appeared to him to be an eminently sensible plan, and so, leaving enough cash on the table to cover their consumption, they left. Jumping into a taxi, she took him to a much more civilised establishment, with live music, and more easy-going clientele. They chatted over drinks, and he found her to be charming company. Soon thereafter they retired to his hotel. They kissed and embraced, and then stripped off. Naked he could see how truly beautiful she was, a long-limbed, powerful Amazon, with a radiant smile to match. They lay down on the bed, and kissed passionately before he started to explore further afield. She had fantastic breasts, not over-large but perfectly in harmony with the rest of her body. Slowly he continued his descent, lingering around her muscular belly where he kissed her belly button, below which was a tuft of curly black hair. But when he wanted to descent to the depths, she pulled him back up, and enjoined him to enter her.

Quickly he grabbed his condom from his wallet and tugged it on, before returning to the chase. But somehow it had a dampening effect, constituting a barrier between their intimacy and mutual pleasure. It was like fucking a kitchen glove. Finally she said, "Take it off" and without waiting for an answer, pulled herself back and free and with a swift movement of her hand, removed the offending plastic bag. Then he was back inside her, and immediately appreciated the wisdom of her decision. With each rhythmic thrust he could feel her soft inner tissues give way and accept him, moulding to his shape like living velvet. As he continued he began to get into his stride; but suddenly she turned him over and sat on him. Her heavy bulk provided enough resistance for him to push against, and it wasn't long before he was quaking and straining to the animal rhythm of a gratifying orgasm.

They were colleagues, and after celebrating New Year's Eve together, ended up at his place. After sitting and talking together for hours on the beach, until the first shades of the next day began to spread into the sky, it seemed like the logical thing to do. She said she would stay the night, and wanted to go to bed straight away. Confused as to the nature of their relationship, he was rather slow on the uptake, until she commanded him to join her. She was a well-built girl, muscular rather than fat, with a beautiful smile. In the first light he admired the harmonious contours of her body, shaped by God to travel this earth. He kissed her, and she indicated that she wanted straight sex, straight away. He was happy to oblige, and quickly he reached orgasm, pulling out at the last moment to cast his seed on to her warm, smooth stomach.

They became friends and met up regularly, at weekends and in the evenings, when they were able to dedicate more time and energy to their mutual enjoyment of each other. She liked to say "Fuck me" in English, even though it wasn't her language. She also told him to either use a condom, or ejaculate inside her. Exploring her hidden delights on one occasion, he slid a forefinger up her arsehole, which made her jump away from him with a "No!" Her favourite activity was straight sex, which she enjoined him to engage in at length, commanding him to labour through her fanny-farts and save up his orgasm until she was ready to enjoy hers. After intense sessions of fucking her he was often left out of breath and in a sweat, with a sore cock. One day at work she came into his office with a note that said "Meet me outside in five minutes". He did so, and she encouraged him to take time off work to go with her to a nearby motel. As he had nothing urgent on that day, he did so. She had arranged everything, and they retired to a small hut with a bed that was hardly big enough for the two of them. But the knowledge that he should have been at work played on his mind and prevented him giving full rein to his passions, with the result that it was not one of their longest sessions. He also got to know her sister, who she did not get on with, and who was almost as pretty; but he was unable to persuade her to engage in the same activities as her sibling.

One evening he got very drunk in a café, and found himself in the company of three very pretty young ladies, two of whom indicated they were inclined to continue socialising with him in the intimacy of his home. However, they would not go together, and asked him to choose which one would do him the honour. Inspecting them both as he cuddled them, he was unable to make such a drastic and potentially damaging decision, and encouraged them to both come, if only for the company. But eventually a decision was taken out of his hands, and two of his companions departed, leaving one with him. Quickly he paid his bar bill and they drove carefully home. As soon as he had parked and they had entered the house, he led her into the bedroom where they stripped off and got into the bed. They seemed to hit it off immediately, the sexual urges of their bodies complementing the friendship they had already established to create a unique chemistry. He kissed her breasts and genitals at length, engendering profound appreciation if not ecstasy in his companion. Then he returned to the lying position beside her, and they kissed amid the laughter of a shared joke before he mounted her and they had passionate, straight sex. Their rocking movements transferred to the bed, but he was not distracted as he gradually built up to a great orgasm, during which she hugged him all the tighter. After that there was nothing for it but to fall asleep, and indulge in another round of fornication in the morning light. He never saw her or her friend again, and sought for them in vain.

One night he had returned to his solitary digs after imbibing more than a few beers in the small town's watering holes. Having just verified that there was nothing of interest on the TV, he was just contemplating going to bed when there was a knock on the door. The sixth sense that sometimes manifests itself on the periphery of inebriation suddenly sent a powerful if incoherent message into his psyche, and immediately hard and his head swimming, he stood up and opened the door. It was a young woman he didn't recognise, smiling and asking if she could come in. Without a word he stepped back and allowed her to pass. Closing the door behind him, he indicated that she should sit in the armchair, which she did. Glancing at her again, he ascertained that she was quite young, but he had no memory of having seen her before. Kneeling before her, again without a word, he ran his hands up her legs and, undoing her trousers, he tugged them off. She seemed surprised, but also suddenly very excited, as she assisted his efforts with a few gentle kicks. He then returned his hands to her waist, and grasping the top hem of her knickers, pulled them down her legs. This time he could sense her sexual excitement. Having thus prepared the way, he slid his hands under her buttocks and pulled her crotch forward, before starting to administer the kiss of life. She yielded to his touch and began to emit quiet animal groans. He hair was quite thick, and he had to hold it back to gain full access to her vulva, which he patiently did. He also noticed that her genitalia were quite pungent, indeed fetid, and an alarm bell went off in the back of his intoxicated mind to the effect that he should use a condom if it came to penetration. At least with AIDS you get a 10-year suspended sentence, whereas Ebola is a full stop in ten days flat. After a while he decided he had done his bit, and that it was her turn to warm him up. Lying on his back on the mat on the floor, he bid her approach and perform oral sex on him. She crouched down beside him and began to do so. Her touch was not expert, but she seemed to be enthusiastic, and her performance improved when he instructed her not to use her hands. They were getting into a sustainable passionate rhythm when he bade her crouch over his face. Obediently, she swung one leg over his head, and her pubic area was suddenly before his face. Slowly he encouraged her head movements with some strategic kissing of his own. Then he decided that it was time for the main event and, getting up but bidding her remain in the same pose, he positioned himself behind her and entered her in reverse. She let out a quiet gasp as he pushed right into her, as far as his balls. Grasping her buttocks firmly he proceeded to push in and out, pulling her towards himself with each stroke to achieve the best angle for greatest depth. After only a few minutes, or even moments, he began to feel a powerful force rising within him, constricting his throat and blurring his vision. In an altered state he began to thrust more violently as he ejaculated a jet of spunk deep into her. They got up and he sat on the armchair while she went to the bathroom. When she came back, he told her he was going to bed and that she could take her leave. After she had done so, he had a piss and a shower, and made sure he gave his

cock a good wash. He never saw her again, and
never found out who she was.

VI

"The war in the Middle East has been raging for 15 years. Three once stable and prosperous countries have been reduced to destitution and lawlessness, and the poorest country in the region is undergoing starvation and the worst cholera epidemic ever recorded. The very notion of Islamic society has been thrown into absolute flux."

He picked her up as a hitch-hiker one evening. It had just been raining hard, and he took pity on the female form clad in a long black dress sheltering under the eaves of a large tree that extended over a high wall into the road. The position he had to stop in on the busy road meant that it was not possible to approach the passenger door from the pavement without stepping into a potentially very deep puddle. "What do I do?" she called. "Get in the back" he shouted back, leaning backwards and opening the door. After an initial hesitation, she managed to reach the open doorway and climbed in. She seemed very pleased to see him, and began to hug him from behind in a very amiable fashion as he drove off. After a while he encouraged her to clamber into the passenger seat, from whence it would be much easier for them to get to know each other. She did so, and he noticed she was very pretty, albeit a good ten years his junior. They stopped for a drink in a couple of watering holes, one he knew, one her choice, before retiring to his flat. At her lead they went straight up to the bedroom. Without any encouragement from him she undressed and got into bed, as did he. Her young form was beautiful on the eye, and to the touch, as he quickly discovered. After some introductory kissing, she encouraged him to mount her, in which position she guided his cock into her. Her soft body seemed to yield to his every motion and offer only mutual pleasure in return. After he had orgasmed with pleasure, he indicated to her that he needed to sleep. Somewhat disappointed, she turned her back and quickly they were both out for the count. They awoke early in the morning, and there was just time for a reprise of the evening's activities before she had to go home to get ready for work.

They became good friends, and met up often, usually at the weekend. He quickly discovered that she preferred penetration from behind. Her favourite place for it was on the couch. When he was fucking her she kept looking back at him, which after a while he used to find off-putting. On one occasion he attempted to perform oral sex on her, but she found it an alien concept, and seemed unable to spread her legs widely enough to allow him to engage with her vulva. She had a go doing the same to him, but beyond putting his cock in her mouth she didn't seem to get it. One evening they went out for a drink in his car. On the way back, she asked him to drive to a deserted area. Parking up, she asked him to fuck her there and then. He clambered over into the passenger seat, managed to push it back, and as she lifted her skirt and took her knickers off, he pulled his trousers down. To his surprise, they managed in the cramped space to achieve a satisfactory degree of traction, and as his thrust became quicker and more powerful, she enjoined him to come inside her. He did so to their mutual intense pleasure a few breathless instants later, not least because he did not fancy having to clean it up.

One evening, encouraged by his previous experience, he picked up another female hitchhiker. This time she had accosted him as he returned to his parked vehicle, and asked him to drive her to the peninsula. She was very sensual in her approach.

He couldn't tell whether or not she was local, but he bade her enter his vehicle. At first she appeared somewhat taciturn. But as they drove along she suddenly stripped off in the passenger seat. This was a distraction to his driving, and she encouraged him to pull over in a hotel car park. After he had parked in a secluded corner, he pulled his trousers down, and she offered to "suck" him, to which he consented. His initial idea had been to allow her to warm him up, and then to have full sex in the car. But she was so skilful in her hands-free application that before he knew it, he was coming right into her mouth. She kept on sucking until, having run dry, he stopped her. Rather ungracefully, she opened the door and spat his seed onto the stony ground.

They worked in the same office, and he invited her out to dinner one evening. She was petite and not exactly beautiful, but exuded a powerful female sexuality that he found irresistible. Her walk, purposeful with swaying hips, seemed to betray a profound awareness of her own sexual being. She kept him waiting that evening, and he thought she was going to stand him up; but finally she turned up. She said she wasn't hungry, and settled for a dessert while he speedily scoffed the plate he had ordered for himself, eager to move on to the main course that tantalisingly seemed to be promised. After they had both eaten their fill, he suggested she drive him home, as he didn't have a vehicle of his own. She agreed, and when they arrived, he invited her inside for a coffee. She hesitated for a moment before agreeing, and up they went to his upper-floor digs. He entered first, and removing his phone and wallet from his pockets so they wouldn't encumber him, he tossed them strategically onto the armchair and sat on the far end of the couch. He watched as he she went to sit on the armchair and then, seeing it was occupied, sat beside him. After a few minutes of meaningless conversation, he took her by the hands and kissed her. She reciprocated, and soon they were locked in a passionate embrace. He moved closer to her, all the better to kiss her, and placed his hands on her sides. As they continued to snog, he became aware that she was doing something with her hand and, pulling back, noticed that she had undone her shirt and was delicately caressing her right nipple. She had extracted the breast from her bra. Not one to miss an obvious cue like that, he bent down, rather awkwardly because of their position, and began to suck and kiss her breast. It was a dark brown colour, and seemed to contrast starkly with her light skin. As he worked on her he heard her begin to emit short gasps and stifled groans. Pulling back to reposition himself, he noticed this time to his surprise that she had hitched up her short denim skirt and had her left hand inside her knickers, and was slowly but surely masturbating. Quickly he knelt down in front of her and, pulling her knickers off, he plunged his face into the mass of black public hair to give her the satisfaction she appeared to crave. But here was yet another surprise: her bush was so thick, and the individual hairs so long, that to gain access to her mucus membrane he had to hold the hair back on each side, using both hands. He almost commented on the extent of her fur he was so surprised, but checked himself in time. The way now being clear, he began to gently traverse the smooth expanse between her clitoris and the entrance to the holy of holies. She seemed to appreciate his efforts, as she subsided in her seat, pushing her hips forward to facilitate his efforts, all the while letting out incoherent vocal expressions of enjoyment. He began to worry that his flatmate, a gay student, would be disturbed in his solitary confinement. But now he decided that things had reached the point of no return, and standing up, he led her by the hand to his room. His only dilemma was whether to lift her denim skirt up again, or to tug it off.

She was an air hostess. When he asked her for a glass of water in mid-flight, she brought it together with a piece of paper bearing her phone number. As soon as he was ensconced in his hotel, he phoned her and they agreed to meet the following evening. They went out for dinner and had what he judged to be a good time, but he was unsure whether to invite her back to his hotel, and in the end they said good night on the street.

She met up again the next time he was in town, and she came to his hotel in the afternoon (it was the weekend). This time he could tell she was on for it. They sat side by side on the bed and talked, and he took an almost cruel pleasure in observing her attempts to initiate physical contact. In the end he just kissed her, and she reciprocated passionately. After some time he began to undress her slowly, first her top, which was the cue for some kissing and caressing of her breasts. Then he removed the rest of her clothing, savouring the moment when, after the trousers had gone, the knickers were slowly pulled down to reveal her holy of holies to him for the first time. She was so petite she was almost like a child, with tiny breasts and only a trace of public hair above her oriental crotch. She was now lying on the bed, and he dutifully went down on her, savouring the gentle, yielding smoothness of her inner sanctum. His head began to swim with the excitement, and after a while he had to rise up again and mount her. She was very tight, and had to facilitate his entry with her hand and some repositioning of her hips, all of which threatened to unleash his orgasm. But he was able to hold on, and after a few strokes, withdrew again, this time to ejaculate on her stomach.

They started to see each other regularly, and the next time she invited him to her parents' flat (they were away), and encouraged him to fuck her on their bed. He wasn't too keen on the associations, but she was not to be resisted. She acquiesced to his oral ministrations, but what she really enjoyed was straight sex. Alas, her vagina was so tight that prolonged activity was hard work, and once caused him a lesion on his cock. She being so light, it was as if there was nothing to hold onto and simply fuck when his vision started to blur as a prelude to orgasm. But it was a pleasure to see her beautiful face looking at him while she slid effortlessly up and down his cock as he lay on his back. He once turned her round and penetrated her from behind, but she complained that she found that position painful and preferred the missionary. Between her tiny buttocks he caught a glimpse of her arsehole, a delightful centre of the universe, a tight introspective maelstrom. Strictly no entry.

They met briefly at work, and in a random conversation she indicated that she liked him. He saw her later in the day, and suggested they meet up that evening in his hotel. She agreed, and that evening they met up and had a drink in the hotel lounge. She was very beautiful, tall and angular, with blonde hair. As they walked towards the lift to ascend to his room he was struck by the apparent conflict between her innocent demeanour, and her intention, he hoped, of engaging in intimate activity with him. No sooner had they entered his room than he received a business phone call, that he could not put off. As he spoke, he bade her sit on the bed, and at the same time started to remove his clothes. Taking her cue from him, she stripped off. Nevertheless, he was forced to focus his attention on the phone call, as it concerned an operational matter that required an immediate response. When he was finally able to hang up, she was completely naked on the bed, smiling at him. He noticed immediately that her body was totally hairless. Removing the rest of his clothes, he lay down beside her, and they kissed passionately. He started to kiss and caress her firm breasts, which were flawless in their round perfection. Inevitably he then progressed downwards, stroking and kissing her warm, flat. smooth stomach. She seemed to appreciate his efforts, as she let out quiet groans. When he finally positioned himself in front of the golden gate, he found it to be perfectly smooth and soft. Gently her parted her lips with his tongue, and began to tease her clitoris and the entrance to the inner sanctum. Pushing inside from time to time, he discovered that it subtle taste was truly delightful. Next, he went down lower still and began to gently explore her anus with his tongue. This immediately provoked a gasp of pleasure, which was sustained when he began to massage her vulva from the top with his forefinger. Her feet were still flat on the bed. The whole experience was so erotic that he feared it was unsustainable. "Do you want me to use a condom?" he asked her. "It's up to you" she replied with a smile. Alas, while deliberating which option was best, the sheer perfection of her body became too much for him to bear, and he shot his load then and there on the bedsheets. They didn't meet up again.

VII

"The heart of darkness is to be found not on the ground where evil deeds are done, but within the great institutions where feckless fascists and fornicators accumulate privilege inside a protective bubble."

He had gone out to buy some maps, and had been told there was a suitable business just down the road, on the second floor, hidden from the hustle and bustle of the main road. Stepping off the pavement, he followed the directions he had been given, and soon found the place. But there seemed to be no-one there. "Hello" he called, and in answer a pretty young woman with a glint of mischief in her eye appeared from within. At the same time, he heard another woman's voice, and looking through the open door from whence it had come, saw another young lady clad in the same while shirt and blue skirt, get up from the floor where she had evidently been sleeping. This was all material for a few humorous comments from him, and soon he and the second woman, also pretty, were engaged in a flirtatious conversation. He tried to encourage the first girl to join in, but she appeared to be rather taciturn, at least in the company of her friend. When he had finished his business, the more forward lady passed him her phone number; he wanted to ask for her friend's too, but thought he should not try to take a mile when he had already been given an inch. He also thought he could come back later and get her number. Later that day, he called the number, and his new friend agreed they should meet the following afternoon, which was a Saturday. He wasn't entirely sure she would turn up, but at the allotted time the phone in the room rang, and reception informed him he had a visitor waiting downstairs. He hurried down to see her, and suggest they have a drink in the bar, but she urged him towards the lift, "before anyone sees me". It transpired that she was engaged. They went up to his room, a palpable sense of anticipation growing between them in the lift. He bade her sit on the bed, and he sat on the armchair, intending to let her take the lead. They engaged in some small talk, during which she quizzed him on his sexual habits, including whether he always used a condom, and whether he enjoyed oral sex. Then finally she said, "Do you want to fuck me or not?", to which he replied in the affirmative. She said she wanted to have a shower first, and he pointed the bathroom out to her. While she was showering, he stripped off, and waited for her still seated on the armchair. Finally she came out, holding a towel around her. "What's that for?" he asked, "You said we were going to fuck". In answer she cast the towel aside, revealing all her beauty to him. She was pretty enough, although her legs appeared to be somewhat short in proportion to her upper body, and he noted to himself that she had been more attractive the day before, fully dressed in her office. But standing up, he led her to the bed, and they began to kiss passionately, sitting on the edge. After some time he pushed her back onto the bed and transferred his attention to her breasts. Her nipples were like little dark buds. "Go down on me" he suddenly heard her say, and with a surprised look at her, he did just that. He outer lips parted to reveal the delicate folds inside, and he used his tongue to explore her clitoris, occasionally thrusting it into her vagina, and gently massaging the space in between. He had the impression that she was observing his every move. Finally he heard her issue another command: "That's enough". He got up, and leaning over and extracting a condom from her handbag, she proffered it to him. He quickly opened the sachet and unrolled the artificial membrane onto his cock, and then mounted her. With a few deft movements of her hand he was inside her, and began to thrust back and forth. Her warm body was still wet in places where she hadn't dried herself properly after her shower, which was both a distraction and an exciting new sensation. Again he had the impression that she had a detached view of his performance and was not really getting carried away, and so after a while he decided to make the most of it, and in a few violent shoves he orgasmed. When he withdrew, she insisted on examining the condom before he went to the bathroom to remove it and wash his cock (and piss). Upon his return he asked her if she was satisfied with the experience. "It was alright" she commented. He then suggested they meet up again, with her friend from work. "Contact her yourself if you like her" she replied, although she said she might call him again the next day.

She worked as a waitress in a café where he would often have lunch, sometimes alone, sometimes with colleagues. He remarked her beauty the first day he saw her – voluptuous, with an angelic face, and an enchanting smile. At first she paid no heed to his compliments, but when he left a note on the table asking for her phone number, she wrote it down for him. He phoned her and they met up that afternoon. After some initial pleasantries, which included a walk on the beach and then a seat on a sun-bleached tree trunk, when she pulled up her skirt to reveal white knickers, and then pulled them down to reveal a brown, shaved fanny, they agreed that it would be opportune if she were to visit him in his hotel that evening. She came round at the appointed time, and as soon as they were alone in his room, they kissed passionately and at length while hugging each other. He realised that there was something about her that had awoken a sentimental feeling in his breast. Quickly they got undressed, and she said she wanted to have a shower. He suggested they shower together, and they both managed to fit into the confined cubicle. He was then able to feast his eyes on her well-proportioned, voluptuous form, the shaved pubic hair revealing the modest entrance to her earthly delights. He was getting very excited, but didn't want their rendezvous to end in a fumbled encounter in these uncomfortable surroundings. They lathered each other with soap and then rinsed each other off before returning to the bedroom. They got on the bed, and again started to kiss passionately. He enjoyed her embrace, and continued to kiss her for some time, savouring every moment before descending to kiss her breasts. After her while he continued his slow descent, lavishing his affections on her stomach and her belly button, before entering the zone between her legs. Her vulva was set quite far back, and was very small, even deformed. He didn't ask her about it in case she was unaware, but contented himself with entering her vagina with his tongue, which she seemed to appreciate. She let out a more powerful gasp when he descended a degree further and thrust his tongue up her anus, which he was pleased to discover opened willingly to his touch. But more powerful forces were overtaking him and, returning to her position, he mounted her and entered her vagina. She raised her legs and spread her hips, which facilitated his entry and allowed him to push deep into her with his first thrust. Despite his intention to make the experience last, it wasn't long before his rhythmic strokes unleashed an electrical storm in his brain and he was lost in an orgasmic flood. After he had caught his breath he went to the bathroom to wash his cock. They talked and watched TV together for a while, she sitting with her legs up on the armchair in what struck him as a very beautiful pose. He embraced her from behind, caressing her arms and breasts while he kissed her, and then encouraging her to get up, led her back to the bed. This time he encouraged her to crouch on all fours on the edge of the bed, while he stood on the floor and entered her from behind. The feeling was exquisite has he thrust into her with rhythmic strokes, at first slow and then gradually accelerating, grasping her firm, black buttocks with both hands, and periodically exchanging glances with her as she looked back at him with an angelic expression from time to time. They played this game of give and take for some time until finally, having put off the conclusion several times, he decided it was time for the grand finale. Speeding up, he started to push into her with increasing violence, the slap of flesh against flesh playing counterpoint to their gasps and groans, until he came deep into her, continuing his strokes until he felt he had run dry. After he had come back to earth and withdrawn from her embrace, they heard a loud plop as a wad of his spunk marinated in vaginal juices fell out of her onto the bed frame. In the middle of the night he woke up and wanted to fuck her again; she was lying with back to him, but when he tried to turn her over she muttered "Leave me alone".

They met up regularly, whenever they could. On the next occasion, after once again exploring her vagina with his tongue, he decided he would pay more attention to her arsehole. Again thrusting his tongue up her black hole, he noted with anticipation that it had some room to manoeuvre. He pushed his finger up it as he returned to licking her fanny, and noted that it slid in without resistance. But when he stood up and tried to push his cock in, she objected with, "Do you want to hurt me?" Reluctantly he then pushed into her vagina and they had passionate, albeit short-lived straight sex. Afterwards she got up and went to the bathroom. Lying on the bed and catching his breath, he thought he heard the sound of solid matter dropping into water, and then a farting noise. Dismissing it, he continued his meditations on life and love until he suddenly caught the unmistakable whiff of shit. She could at least have closed the bathroom door! It was probably just as well that they hadn't had anal sex, as she might have shit all over the bed, as he recalled from an anecdote had happened to a colleague once. When she returned they were silent for a while, and then she asked, "Everything alright?" to which he just shrugged. In the middle of the night, he was again taken by the desire to fuck her, and this time, when he attempted to roll over, she just complied, but without opening her eyes. He mounted and entered her, supporting himself on his fists on the mattress in order not to wake her, and embarked immediately on a swift, intrusive rhythm. She was dry at first, but he was gratified to feel her vaginal juices quickly start to flow, and before he knew it he had added to them with his own bodily fluids. In the morning he was brushing his teeth when she came into the bathroom, still half asleep, and sat down on the toilet. She leant back with her eyes closed and, splaying her legs on both sides of the bog, just let the piss pour out of her in a powerful jet for what seemed like a long time, all her female mysteries on display in what he couldn't decide was an erotic, a comic or a grotesque posture. If only he'd had his camera to hand.

One of the few places where he could get a drink in the evenings outside his hotel was on the porch of a defunct brothel just down the road. He was sitting there one evening in conversation with the madam when a very forward young lady, touting for business, sat down facing him. Despite his protestations that he was not interested, she continued to hit upon him. Finally she decided to play her trump card and, taking hold of his hand, pushed it up her very short skirt against her crotch. He noticed that her knickers were wet and said, "Your pussy is all wet". "I've just had a piss" she replied.

She was a toilet cleaner at his place of work, very young and beautiful. He met her when he came across her in the gents; thinking he had got the wrong door, he turned to go, but she grabbed him

and encouraged him to go about his business. Her
English was very poor, and he didn't speak her
language. After that they would exchange smiles
whenever their paths crossed. He asked for her
phone number, and told her where he was staying.
That evening he received a confused call from her
and, stepping outside, saw that she had come to see
him. Unsure how to proceed, he took her for a walk
and then tea and cakes, during which they were able
to get to know each other. He very much admired
her lithe and graceful movements, and her beautiful
smile revealing perfect teeth. Before they knew it,
it was time for her to go. Several days later, he
arrived home from work late, to find her waiting
outside his digs. Tired as he was, and deciding that
it was crunch time, he invited her inside. In his
bedroom, he invited her to sit on the armchair, and
he sat opposite her on the bed. They talked for a
while; she was very shy, and after a while he took
off her jacket and hung it on the back of the chair.
Then he encouraged her to sit beside him, which
she did after some hesitation. He put his arm around
her and tried to kiss her, but she hid her face in
shyness. After a while he encouraged her to remove
her headscarf, which she did, placing the pin
carefully on the table and revealing short, but
beautifully braid hair. They went on like this for
some time, engaging in small talk and he
attempting from time to time to move to a new stage
of intimacy. Eventually he suggested they lie down,
and she took up position beside him, face down, and
with her hand on his chest. She told him he had a
son; he was surprised, and had thought she was a
virgin. He could feel an air of contentment

emanating from her, and didn't want to break the spell; and tired as he was, he almost fell asleep. But suddenly rousing himself, he declared it was time for a shower, and undressing himself, encouraged her to do the same. Somewhat taken aback, she nevertheless did so, and they repaired to the bathroom. In the spacious shower he was treated to the natural splendour of her lithe body, her nipples obviously distorted by suckling, her pubic hair unattended but not run wild. She was a true child of nature. After they had soaped and rinsed each other, they returned to the bedroom. From behind he was able to admire her firm, powerful buttocks, and doubted whether they concealed a third entrance. He embraced her from behind and kissed her on the head, neck and shoulders, and she stopped, carried away in a foretaste of ecstasy. Then they got into the bed, under the quilt which was tucked under the mattress, and which he had meant to pull out to give them more freedom of movement. But after 10 days of unrelenting work outside he was quite tired, and had not bothered. He lay beside her and kissed her; she was now completely uninhibited, and smiled at him mischievously with her perfect teeth. But when he slid his hand up her leg she let out a gasp, and when he engaged her fanny and began to massage it, she was already lost in a world of her own. Slowly and gently he continued his caresses, kissing her all the while; and then he descended to increase the intensity of her enjoyment. The tucked up quilt meant he couldn't stretch out fully, but he managed to find a position in which he was between her legs, his mouth level with her genitalia. He began by kissing the pubic hairs on her mound, and then slowly felt his way down with his tongue to her vulva. It seemed to be set quite far back, and was lower down than he expected. As he gently explored her with his tongue, he felt and heard a tremor go through her body. Deciding to go all the way, he began to tease her vulva with his forefinger as he licked her, and then slowly slid his finger down, seeking her anus. Very far down where he judged it should be he felt a gently opening, but it was wet, and slipping the tip of his finger in, he decided that it must be her vagina. By now he was very excited himself, and rather than pursue what was probably a dead end anyway, he rose up to her position and mounted her. His cock slid straight into her vagina, and seemed to go immediately right up to the hilt, at the same time curving down and then up at an unusual angle. The sensation was so intense that he let out a groan, and she cried "I love you!" Then he proceeded to move in and out of her with slow, rhythmic strokes, to their mutual ecstasy. After a while, and in order to delay his climax, he withdrew and turned her over, thinking that fucking her from behind might present him with the opportunity to examine her third eye. But she misunderstood him and lay face down; upon which he crouched over her, and penetrated again. More intense pleasure followed, but he felt it was not quite the right position for orgasm. He exited again, and turning round she indicated that she should sit on top of him, but he said no, and proceeded with the missionary position again. Once again the pleasure was intense, and this time he decided it was time to sprint the final furlong. With increasingly powerful and rapid strokes he reached an orgasm that made his head spin; and then it was all over. Exhausted, he just lay beside her catching her breath, while she made herself comfortable among the pile of surplus pillows that some hotels insist on placing on beds. Just before he went to sleep, he turned towards her and positioned himself so that he was lying half on top of her and half on the curtains, he legs spread on either side of him. In that position they both fell asleep, and any notions he had of a midnight repeat of their love-making came to nought, as they both slept in the next morning, and she had to leave as soon as they woke up.

He saw her again over the next few days at work, exchanging furtive but tender glances and smiles, but they never had the opportunity to be alone together again.

There were several young women sitting at the bar as he entered. He looked them over as he ordered a drink, and one of them in particular, a blonde, was very pretty. He approached her from behind and started to chat her up. She turned her head towards him and responded to his advances positively; but it was only when she stood up that he noticed her stomach was huge. "How many months?" he asked. "Seven" she replied, and stepping back, lifted her shirt to reveal a dial painted on her stomach with the needle indicating three quarters, and the inscription above "70% full". When he returned to the bar, another young lady, rather plump, but pretty enough, began to lavish her attentions on him. But he had noticed when he entered the bar that she had been in the company of an elderly man, who had now made himself scarce. He wasn't sure whether he was her boyfriend, her pimp, or her father - or perhaps all three, so he rebuffed her politely.

He was killed in a freak accident in a slaughter house in Fort Worth, Texas, in 1998.

"I have carefully gathered what I have been able to discover about him, and it is presented here for your perusal. No doubt you will admire his spirit and character, and even shed a tear for his fate."

Johann Wolfgang Goethe, *The Sorrows of Young Werther*

www.ingramcontent.com/pod-product-compliance
Lightning Source LLC
Chambersburg PA
CBHW031353060726
47590CB00007B/2763